by Lynn Rowe Reed

Basil's Birds

Marshall Cavendish Children

Copyright © 2010 by Lynn Rowe Reed

All rights reserved

Marshall Cavendish Corporation

99 White Plains Road

Tarrytown, NY 10591

www.marshallcavendish.us/kids

Thanks to Brian Art for photographing the bird's nest
that appears in the art throughout the book.

Library of Congress Cataloging-in-Publication Data

Reed, Lynn Rowe.

Basil's birds / by Lynn Rowe Reed. — 1st ed.

p. cm.

Summary: While Basil the school janitor is napping, birds build a nest atop
his head and when the eggs hatch, he becomes a proud "dad" to the chicks.

ISBN 978-0-7614-5627-8

[1. Nests—Fiction. 2. Birds—Fiction. 3. Janitors—Fiction.] I. Title.

PZ7.R25273Bas 2010

[E]—dc22

2009007071

The illustrations were painted in
gouache on illustration boards.
Many additional items, including
the nest, were scanned or
photographed and added to the
illustrations in Photoshop. The
birds were made in clay, fired,
painted, and scanned.

Book design by Vera Soki

Editor: Margery Cuyler

Printed in Malaysia (T)

First edition

1 3 5 6 4 2

mc Marshall Cavendish
Children

PERCH ELEMENTARY

This book is dedicated to

Russ Garriott and Jane Martin.

On a spring day, the birds around Perch Elementary were looking for places to build their nests. First they began building on the flagpole. Then they began building above the doorway and in the eaves spout.

Principal Kabalsky stepped outdoors to see what was going on.

She immediately sent for the
school janitor, Basil Berkmeister.

Basil Berkmeister
batted the birds
with his broom . . .

. . . until he was so worn out, he fell asleep on the playground.

While he was dozing, the birds came back and found the perfect place to build a new nest.

When Basil woke up, he walked to town for his weekly haircut.

"Just trim around the sides as usual," he told Gustaf the barber. "If you say so," said Gustaf.

Gustaf finished trimming and handed
Basil the mirror.
"Yikes!" said Basil. "I have a bird
on my head!"

Basil didn't know
what to do.

He felt a little sorry
for the bird who had
worked so hard
to build its neat
little home.

And it was
a work of
ART.

Basil went about his usual activities.
At first he was a bit embarrassed.

But soon he found that the nest
was a great conversation piece.

Basil began getting used to the situation. While dining out, he even ordered an extra side dish for the bird.

On Saturday nights, Basil took
his bird to hear some music.

tweet tweet tweet

Then he went to sleep standing up
so as not to disturb the nest.

One morning, Basil
was awakened by little
crackling sounds.
Then the sound of sweet
chirping filled his ears.

Basil was a

DAD!

He announced his wonderful
news to the world.
Everyone congratulated him.
Basil adored his new babies.

He took pictures
and sang lullabies to
them every night.

At the local college, Basil took a class on bird care.

WHAT BIRDS EAT: iNSECTS

He fed his birds
a special diet.

He bathed them
and fluffed their
feathers.

Basil's birds grew
quickly until . . .

. . . one day, they fluttered
and flapped and flew away.

"Come back!" shouted Basil.
"You'll get lost! You'll catch a cold!"

But flying is what birds do,
and these birds flew away.

Basil was very sad. His friends felt sorry for him. Gustaf gave Basil a kitten. The neighbor gave him a hamster. Principal Kabalsky and the kids brought their own pets to visit him.

But nothing helped.

Basil baked a worm pie, hoping the birds would smell it and return home.

WORM PIE

But they didn't.

When spring returned, Basil was especially lonely.

One day, when Basil was outside working . . .

. . . he heard a swoosh of flapping.

Basil looked up
and smiled.